Toots the Cat

Karla Kuskin

Illustrated by

Lisze Bechtold

Henry Holt and Company · New York

Henry Holt and Company, LLC, *Publishers since 1866*
115 West 18th Street, New York, New York 10011
www.henryholt.com

Henry Holt is a registered trademark of Henry Holt and Company, LLC

Library of Congress Cataloging-in-Publication Data
Kuskin, Karla. Toots the cat / Karla Kuskin; illustrated by Lisze Bechtold.—1st ed.
p.   cm.
1. Cats—Juvenile poetry. 2. Children's poetry, American.
I. Bechtold, Lisze. II. Title.
PS3561.U79T66 2005   811'.54—dc22   2004026770
ISBN-13: 978-0-8050-6841-2
ISBN-10: 0-8050-6841-4

First Edition—2005 / Designed by Donna Mark
Printed in the United States of America on acid-free paper. ∞
The artist used pencil, watercolor, and gouache to create
the illustrations for this book.

10 9 8 7 6 5 4 3 2 1

For Toots and Pounce, old friends, RIP —K. K.

For my siblings, Bruce, Robert, Peggy, and Ross —L. B.

Visitor

A cat came down the road mewing.
We gave her milk in a china dish,
some of last night's chicken,
and a few bites of Friday's fish.
She licked her paws and her nose
as if she appreciated what we were doing.
Then she picked a warm spot
in the most comfortable chair
and made it clear
that she had no intention
of ever leaving there.

Toots's Ears

Let us begin with Tootsie's ears,
intelligent
on guard
alert
to any kind of mouse or bird—
a mouse or bird could be dessert.

Her Nose

There is no nose I know,
no nose, I think,
no point as pale and pink,
a rose among fur snows.
If I could choose
to be a snoot as suitable
as it that sits on Toots,
I would have chose to be that very nose.

Her Tail

Following Toots like a boa or banner,
waving farewell in a marvelous manner,
smoke gray and silky,
a billowing sail,
following Toots with a flourish—
her tail.

The Favorite

We have a cat
who looks like night.
Another who is not too bright.
A Siamese who flirts,
the rake.
And Toots,
who walks off with the cake
for cats.
The quickest claws,
the neatest nose.
Our very queen of calicoes,
with four white socks,
all four enclose
Toots's fur-tipped tapping toes
that always go
where Tootsie goes.

In or Out?

When she's in
she meows to be out.
When she's out
she prefers to be in.
Whatever wherever whichever
however forever moreover
from cover to cover
from housemat to clover
she makes it quite clear
she would rather be here
if she's there.

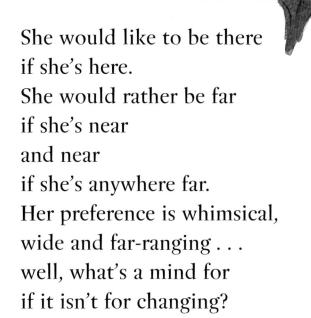

She would like to be there
if she's here.
She would rather be far
if she's near
and near
if she's anywhere far.
Her preference is whimsical,
wide and far-ranging . . .
well, what's a mind for
if it isn't for changing?

Hunting

A bound,
a leap across the lawn
brown birds bob on.
It could be a grass ocean
the way she plows through it
in slow motion.
Ears high,
a bright flame flickering
in each wild, wild eye.
A velvet missile
arching toward a feathered goal.
And cries of "kitty, kitty"
are powerless to halt
the jungle beating
in that small
quite undomesticated soul.

July Cat

Tootsie, you fur ball,
I cry.
The world is aflame
on this day in July.
And you in that cat coat
are hotter than I.
So why,
if you want to be free
of the fur-curling heat,
are you sitting on me?

Summer Afternoon

A sudden sky-high skirmish
of flapping wings
of peeps and cheeps
among the leaf-thick vines.
And fearing mayhem or murder,
I check on Toots,
unconscious and unruffled in her sleep.

Wisterious.

Cats Don't Care What You Wear

Cats don't care
what you wear.
They never are rude
if you're nude.
They may give you a look
with a quizzical purr
as if to say, "Really,
poor creature, no fur.
How awfully embarrassing,
looking like her."
And then add a poker-faced
lingering stare.
"Not that I care," it says.
"Not that I care."

Naps

Cats take naps
from dawn to dawn.
They nap on anything they're on—
a pillow, antique chair, or lawn.
And when their need to nap is gone,
they stretch and yawn
and look around for something else
it might be nice to nap upon.

Toots at Night

Ears back
tail low
toe
by toe
by toe
our Tootsie creeps
looking for a little trouble
while the city sleeps.

The Terrible Cat

The terrible cat of black velvet fur
will leap at your legs
with a thunderous purrrr,
flash through the air
to a lap or a chair,
nibble your dinner,
and probably stare
at your face and your frown
as she daintily tears
the chop you are eating
and swallows it down.

If Tootsie Had Her Way

If Tootsie had her way,
I wouldn't stir.
I wouldn't do my work at all—
I'd work for her.
I'd be her couch,
and she would sit on me all day
and night,
except for little breaks for tuna fish,
which seems to be
the pussycat equivalent
of tea.

Lost Paper

Did you ever spend an hour and forty-eight minutes
looking for a piece of paper
only to realize that
the piece of paper
you have been looking for
for an hour and forty-eight minutes
is underneath the cat?

Mad Cat

We have lost a mad cat
who looked like a raccoon
by the light of the sun,
by the light of the moon,
and though she was willful
and wild as a loon,
she is gone.
It's too soon.
It's too soon.
It's too soon.

Snow Walker

She walks
like a couple of ballerinas
across the bright meringue
of untouched snow
dipping one fine fur foot
first
and then another
while shaking,
de-flaking,
those bright white toes
until
they are free of
bright white snows . . .
just so.

Resting

In a sun pool
like a curled fur shell you lie
breathing light purrs,
inhaling the scene
through one green crescent,
one half-open eye.

When our cat is at rest
our house is at rest
and so is the earth and sky.

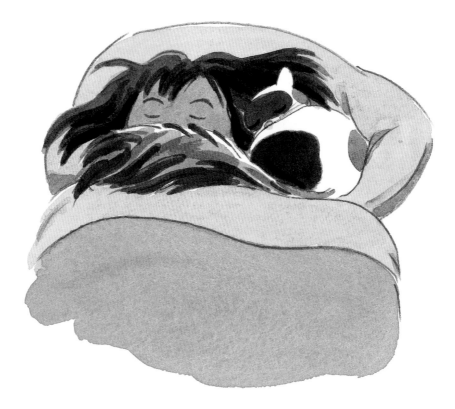